The Italian War As Seen by a Japanese

BY

Harukici Shimoi

Tikhanov Library

Printed and produced in Powell River,
British Columbia, Canada.
MMXXI

TO THE OLD FATHERS,
who offered their sons for the sacred name of the
Homeland;
TO THE CHILDREN,
who sent their fathers to the front to avoid having the
flowers of their pastures trampled by the muddy feet of
the barbarians.
TO THE SIMPLE SOLDIERS,
countless nameless Cincinnatus,
who, after the painful life of four years in the trenches,
exposed to all weathers,
now return to the plow, the hammer of yesterday,
content, happy, without any aspiration that their chest
is decorated, if not by the little hands that clasp it with
impetus,
and without any ambition that their names be
remembered by others, except in the blessings of their
elders,
these simple but sincere words
of sympathy and admiration
of a Japanese
I dedicate.

HARUKICI SHIMOI

Naples, March 1919

MEMORY OF WATER AND SOUL

Shimoi, do you remember our race, in the fast and roaring boat, across the gray lagoon, to land at the camp of S. Nicolo where I had my Wings and Arms?

We talked about painful Italy, we talked about our sacrifice, our blood, our desperate days and our unconquered hopes. Do you remember?

All of a sudden I saw two living tears flowing from your impenetrable foreign eyes. And suddenly I recognized you as my brother; and my heart opened.

Now I say to you - on this day of anxious spring - I say to you that no poet of your land ever composed couplets on dew more heavenly than those tears of yours.

X 20 April 1919

Gabriele d'Annunzio

INTRODUCTION

The Professor Harukici Shimoi, author of the following letters from the front lines of our war, teaches Japanese at the Oriental Institute in Naples. He came here at the end of 1915, to replace in this teaching his compatriot, Professor Hidezo Simotomai. The latter was and is a geographer-physicist who, after having traveled through China, southern Africa, America, Scandinavia, England, France and Germany, had come to study the volcanoes of Italy. Here by accident he was called to teach Japanese at the Oriental Institute of Naples, but essentially he was my assistant at the Institute of Physical Geography at the University of Naples, and together with me for a couple of years he traveled and studied the volcanoes of the Phlegraean Fields and my native mountains of Lucania, in addition to traveling throughout our peninsula, until his return to Japan.

He, a teacher at the University of Sapporo, was adopted as a son by the famous professor of physics at the University of Tokyo, A. Tanakadate, so that he is now called, no longer Simotomai, but Hidezo Tanakadate. But, even under his new name, he retains unchanged the nostalgia and deep affection for our country that he seems to have transmitted to his successor, Harukici Shimoi. Both Shimoi and Tanakadate are two model representatives of Japan. Simotomai, descendant of an ancient, noble family, whose legendary deeds are still represented in Japanese theaters, is tall, thin, delicate in appearance, but extremely resistant to fatigue and very agile in the most perilous alpine ascents. Shimoi, also descending from a family of samurai, son of a talented architect, is small, short, robust, and also endowed with extreme physical and moral energy. Both short-sighted, both armed with golden glasses, both in love, as much as one can be in love, with Italy.

Simotomai came to this love for Italy by degrees, through experience. He, endowed with a scientific spirit, after having travelled around the world for scientific instruction, arrived for the purpose of geographical and geological studies in Italy, and here, after having known and loved the mountains and the volcanoes, he knew, studied and loved the landscape and the inhabitants and their history and their art so that he finished his studies among my native mountains of Lagonegro with the feeling to be almost in his native land, and has kept so deep the nostalgia of our country, that now from his country he often yearns to return to Italy, which appears to him as his second home, spiritually.

Shimoi instead came directly from Japan to Italy. But he, endowed with an artistic spirit, already knew and loved Italy in his native country; for him embodied in its greatest representative, Dante.

From Dante he had learned the Italian language, for Dante he had founded in Japan a society named after him, to Dante he was having his architect father build a house and a library in Tokyo.

So when the opportunity arose for him to come to Dante's homeland, he embarked without hesitation and crossed thousands of miles of sea to reach the sacred soil of Italy.

Here he arrived, as I have said, at the end of 1915 and for more than three years he dedicated all his energies to the study and understanding of our country; of which he now knew everything, from the Alps to Etna, from the Adriatic to the Tyrrhenian Sea, from the most splendid monuments to the bleakest countryside, from the highest intellectual and social peaks to the lowest strata of the population. Gifted with an exquisite artistic sensibility and a vivid and noble force of expression, he received in his mind countless visions of our land and our people and he has captured them, with the brush and the pen, in paintings, sketches, and writings, which will bring to the land of the Rising Sun the image of a living and vibrant Italy, which has many points of contact with the beautiful land of Dai Nippon.

In these three years Shimoi has lived the intimate tragedy of the war and wanted to take part in the last act of it, on the Piave, to see, study and understand closely the soul of the Italian people in its most humble representatives, especially the peasants, whether they were still working in the fields as old men, women and children, or fighting as adults in the muddy and dusty gray-green uniform of the infantryman in the trenches.

In the months of October and November he was always in the front line, with the Italian soldiers, and from there, in the moments of rest, he wrote me the letters, which now his friend Gherardo Marone wanted to collect in this volume. I invite the young Italians to read them. They are the most beautiful and moving homage paid to Italy by a son of that land of artists, warriors and ascetics that produced in General Nogi the most shining example of military virtue.

Senator G. De Lorenzo

THE ITALIAN

WAR

AS

SEEN

BY A

JAPANESE

SAMURAI.

LETTER FROM SEN. G. DE LORENZO

Naples, September 24, 1918

Dear Shimoi,
I am really very pleased with what you are doing for an ever better understanding between Italy and Japan, two countries very similar in so many ways and worthy of understanding each other*, and I find your trip to the front very useful for such a highly spiritual purpose. I hope that you will find noble hearts there, worthy of admiration and love in Japan as well.

The most cordial wishes and greetings from

your affectionate
G. De Lorenzo

---

* The Senator speaks of the negotiations that I have prepared between the Italian and Japanese governments.

LETTER FROM S.E.F.S. NITTI
The Minister of the Treasury.
Rome, September 27, 1918

Dear Captain,
Prof. H. Shimoi, distinguished Japanese writer and sincere friend of Italy, has come to you. With letters and telegrams he enlightens public opinion in Japan as well.

I will be grateful if you will introduce him to General Diaz and if you will find a way to make him visit our front with every care. I believe that, in all respects, your visit will be useful in making our war and its difficulty known in Japan.

With the most cordial greetings,
most affectionately Nitti
Hon. Captain Giovanni Visconti Venosta
Particular Secretary of H.E. Gen. Etas.

PADOVA

30 Ottobre 1918

Train of women and children

When I left Bologna, my first surprise was the train. A train going to the front and, more importantly, to the war zone! I thought all trains were loaded with proud soldiers going to the line and groaning wounded returning. The truth is, however, that the train was full of women and children returning to their homes - the children singing incessantly and the women chatting happily, with a distinct Veneto accent. It gave me the impression of one of those excursion trains of childhood gardens that are often made in Japan in the spring. It was really the scene of a train on a pleasure trip!

I hoped for more

At the Supreme Command Press Office, however, I was very disappointed. As soon as I arrived, I explained the purpose of my trip, but they wanted to treat me like all the foreign missions that were rushing through the Italian front. That is, they wanted me to know about the Italian war, while I wanted to see it; they gave me abstract explanations, while I wanted the real sensations.

For example, one day, when I went to Monte Grappa, I saw a cave dug into the rock with a rough wall of planks, with a sign outside, "POST". There was a mailbox, and a soldier, leaning on the rock, was attentively reading a letter - perhaps a dear letter that had arrived from afar a few minutes earlier.

Back in Padua, I asked the Chief of the Press Office to let me visit a post office at the front, to see the arrivals, distributions and dispatches of the military mail, I wanted to see and describe a scene from life.

After five days, - you know, Mr. Senator, what did you prepare for me? - the Chief called me and said: "In a few days I will take you to Bologna. You can have all the news of the postal service in the war zone; even that of the front. A mail from the line is a trifle." This is the way of treatment.

When I asked permission to visit an elementary school in a town very close to the firing line, the Chief pointed out to me an inspector from the school section of a town hall.

On my return from Monte Grappa, I saw a young wounded soldier feeding a small white dog on the road. A dog in the valley, amidst the rumbling of cannon fire, playing with a wounded brave is a beautiful picture. I wanted to stop the car, but the officers who were guiding me said: "No; that's nonsense!" If I had been able to stop the car, I could have collected the news to prepare an article on a poetic episode of war that, along with the soldier's name and the dog's name, would be known proverbially to all the boys in Japan.

I explained and explained my wish to the Chief, and finally despaired completely of the possibility of persuading the military.

Fear of what?

At the top of Mount Colmareggio, there is a lonely house of a farmer who has four children, all under ten years. The children were playing, innocent, with the soldiers, in the face of deafening cannon fire.

"Aren't you afraid?" I asked them.

"Afraid of what?" And they looked at me in amazement.

"Afraid of war."

"Why?"

"If the enemies come."

"No, here are our soldiers" And they looked up at the soldiers who were caressing them smiling.

What beautiful confidence!

Children do not doubt that, as long as there is an Italian soldier at their side, the enemies can never come.

Heroes without a name

On the same day, in the village of Maser, below the hills of Asolo, I saw a moving scene. It was Sunday. In the deserted square in front of the half-destroyed church, a stooped old man with white hair walked toward the church. At his sides were two young soldiers at rest, walking together supporting him,

It was not a pretty picture!

I am looking for these beautiful and moving scenes, which so many heroes, young and old, perform every day without being remembered by anyone. It is not only the decorated and praised and applauded heroes that make me admire them. I have equal admiration for these nameless heroes as well.

The shoulders of a Japanese

After the beginning of the offensive, I always find myself on the side where the fighting is fiercest. One day on Mount Grappa under unleashed fire; another day on the other side of the Montello, trying to cross the Piave.

What an infernal fire !

The enemies concentrated their shots on the point where I was anxiously awaiting the adjustment of the military bridge that had been destroyed by enemy fire.

Thick bursts all around me, very close. I saw many who died and who were wounded. I will never forget those two days. A young soldier fell wounded; a piece of shrapnel had entered his right leg, another under the right eye and another in the right ear. . . . .

I approached him and bandaging his leg, I took him on my shoulders and, comforting and encouraging him, I took him to the dressing station. He, feeling bloody, asked me in a low voice for my name. I told him simply: "A Japanese, a lover of Italy." What does it matter to hear Shimoi's name? I'd be happier to let him know that the shoulders of a Japanese had given him support!

Under the wild firing to harass the passage of our troops, we waited until the evening in vain.

Crossing the Piave

The next day, however, with cold courage, I attempted the crossing of the Piave in a boat, because the bridge, fixed during the night, had been destroyed again.

What a manly excitement! Passing a current with a speed of 2.50 meters per second, in an iron boat, under the tremendous blows of the enemy!

I am proud to be able to say that I am the first bourgeois who has passed from the Montello side to the other side of the Piave, to make that first footprint on the reconquered land.

Ah, how many terrible, moving, poetic, cheerful, sad episodes! I could not describe them, not even in ten pages.

I returned to Padua at four o'clock in the morning, all wet, with soaked pants, underpants and socks, because I had forded the currents of the Piave four times. Chilled, I stayed in bed for a day with a fever.

Today I feel better, although I still have a cough. Tonight I will leave again for the line of fire. Since the car still cannot cross the Piave, I will walk the entire eighty kilometer trip, sleeping on the road or in the field or under the destroyed wall of some little house. I want to stay on this side until I can see the water of the Tagliamento, then a visit to Pasubio and Adamello; and then to my *bella Napoli*.

In the meantime, please accept, along with the family of S.E. Nitti, the most cordial greetings from

Your friend,
Harukiei Shimoi

Note

To justify my complaint about the treatment of the Press Office, I add here the letter that Mr. Gnelfo Civinini of the Corriere della Sera, wrote to recommend me to Major Maurizio Rava, head of the Photo-Cinematic-Graphic Section of the Supreme Command.

Dearest Major,

Our friend Prof. Shimoi has a great desire to follow the events of these days a little closer. At the Press Office, they have not understood anything of what he is, of what he counts, of what interests him. And they leave him to hang around the cafés of Padua while he wants to get to know our trenches. And they give him information, while he wants to know about sensations.

Can't you take him under your wings? He would be delighted to have one of your teams, as our American colleague J. Hare has often done. See if you can satisfy him. And thank you.

Many kind regards.
Your Civinini
Major Maurizio Rara.

And I thank sincerely Mr. Major, for his kindness shown to me at the moment of the presentation, with his warm promise that, at the first occasion, I will have the pleasure to be accompanied by a team of his Section, although this promised occasion never came to me, while the nicknamed Mr. Mare had several times the fortune to meet at the occasion, during the great offensive that came after this welcome promise.

LETTER OF SEN, G. DE LORENZO
Naples, November 2, 1918

Dear Shimoi,

I was worried about your long silence, after the first postcards sent to me from the front, when I received your long letter of October 30 (which I read to the Nitti family and to Admiral Millo) which brought me your beautiful and vivid impressions of the war. Write to me more often and at greater length, which will give me great pleasure, and have many greetings from the family of S.E. Nitti and from

Your affectionate
G. De Lorenza

PADOVA
5 Novembre 1918

Honorable Senator De Lorenzo,

Having just received your welcome, I immediately set about writing you another long letter, encouraged by your indulgent words, like those of an affectionate father, which assure me that my other one, full of boring repetitions, was not as annoying to you as I feared it would be.

I am only writing you my fragmentary sensations, my various episodes, like the fleeting visions that pass before the eyes of a child who stares fixedly and wonderfully into a kaleidoscope. As for the systematic narratives of all my impressions of these great days that will be eternally remembered, written in golden letters, in the glorious history of

Italy, I want to write them down after my return to Naples, in a complete book, in Italian and Japanese, to be published in Italy and Japan: my homeland that raised me and my second homeland which fills me with life.

Not having time for an urgent departure, I did not write anything in my last one about my daring passage of the Piave, by boat, under the fierce fire of the enemy. Back in Padua, at dawn, after a day and night of impending dangers and great joy, I cried out happily: "I have lived a day !"

It is of that day that I want to describe some episodes.

Terror of war

Most will never know the experience of seeing a field of corpses, not a few, but innumerable, on the vast bed of the Piave, as in front of military bridge B, under the monumental Montello, from where the troops of the VIII Army, commanded by General Caviglia, who was in Japan and Manchuria during the Russo-Japanese war, passed with heavy losses as military attaché.

At one point, you couldn't cross the riverbed except by stepping on the dense piles of flesh and bone rolling in blood.

That's the terror of war!

Pain of war

I spent the day in the trench of the advanced line on the other side of the Piave, among the Arditi who had passed the river first, and after sunset, on a foggy evening, in the thick darkness, illuminated every now and then by the glow of searchlights and the bursts of grenades, I set off, led by a Neapolitan captain who had studied at the University of Naples and who knew Seimotomai personally.

We walked silently, in the thick fog, through fields and woods where no path could be found.

And during this exciting walk, we stopped suddenly at the heartbreaking moans coming from the depths of the darkness. They were serious wounded -

about thirty - abandoned in the vast field, for three days, under the infernal fires of the enemy, without any nourishment.

Moaning, wrenching, dense moaning in the dark! How could I abandon the unhappy ones under fire and in the stiff wind of the river! I am such a man of feeling that such nonsense easily moves me to tears.

"Let's take the two of us, the most seriously wounded among these abandoned people", I said to the Neapolitan captain. But he advised me against it, saying that the bridge would be rebuilt in a few hours and he would notify the health of the army corps as soon as it arrived on the other side of the river.

The walk in the dark, under the continuous bursts of grenades and shrapnel was so tiring that I, obedient to the captain's words, left the disconsolate wounded with words of encouragement.

This is the pain of war!

Beauty of war

After a while, a trembling voice with a foreign accent called to us. The voice came from below the bank, where we were walking mute. They were two Austrians, prisoners, also abandoned in this vast confusion of the hurricane of the offensive. The two prisoners, wounded, without eating for three days, had taken shelter under the bank, together with an Italian soldier who had been seriously wounded. And these two Austrians had cared for him for three days - three days and three nights, which must have seemed like an eternity to them - like affectionate nurses.

The bitter war that calls for blood and slaughter and destroys nations, races and civilizations, sometimes takes place miraculously, as in this case, removing the difference of race, nationality and language, to tighten the adversaries in a sublime affection, not only of friends, but of brothers.

Enemies caring for a wounded Italian, heedless of the constant dangers to themselves, is a beautiful irony of the bloody battle. —Don't you think so, Mr. Senator?

This is the humanitarian beauty of war!

Poetry of War

After having passed many times, by ford, the currents, we arrived at the place where the soldiers of the genius were striving, like madmen, to build the bridge under the enemy shots.

Night was already high.

The enormous mass of prisoners, soldiers and Italian officers, impatiently waiting for the bridge to pass, motionless as statues and indifferent to the bangs and rumbles, gave me the impression of a colossal painting by Bataille or, better, of living myself in some fantastic drawing by Doré.

Masses of people, seen wandering in the dark, on the vast bed of the fast flowing Piave - bursts, cannonade, fires, searchlights giving a sinister glow to the black black sky — a field full of corpses, where we had to pass, silent, trampling them — walking in the dark, in woods and wild fields, hearing the groans and the heartbreaks — shadows of soldiers passing in the dark, silent, carrying the wounded — a pause in the tiring path, called by suffering comrades ; — all this seemed to me as if I had found myself in Dante's Inferno. The solemnity, the grandeur of the Divine Poem, I could feel it fully on that evening on the Piave.

This is the Poetry of War!

Deafening silence

"Deafening silence" is a phrase that beautifully expresses the solemnity of combat.

In the midst of the bursts of grenades, of shrapnel, of battery fire, of rifles, of machine guns, which together overwhelm the atmosphere in a deafening roar, there is always a solemn silence that dominates the entire field.

This paradoxical phrase can only be appreciated by those who, reverently, have bowed their heads under the grandiose baptism of fire.

"Pull ! Pull !"

It was the 31st of October.

Informed of the advance of the 3rd Division to the extreme right wing, which had taken place during the night, I left Padua early in the morning,

I wanted to find out about the lively and fresh psychology of the population of the liberated area.

Following the itinerary of Padua - Treviso - Biancade - Fossalto, I arrived at the Piave River, where a military bridge had been built a few hours earlier. The road from the bridge to the camp was not yet made and I had to ask for help from about fifty soldiers who, with two thick ropes, pulled the car from the river bed up to the top of the embankment. You will be able to guess easily that, on one of these ropes, among the cheerful soldiers and among the lively cries of "Pull! Pull!" there were also my hands and my cries.

I like immensely all forms of innocent and childish cries.

A patriotic madman

During the long wait at the right bank of the Piave, I saw a moving scene— moving perhaps only for me.

It was a madman, pale and wispy, apparently little more than twenty years old. He was a young man from a town in the liberated zone. As soon as the long-awaited liberation was accomplished, he went crazy with extreme joy; and grabbing a tricolor flag, he ran to the Piave and, with exultant cries of "Long live Italy!" he crossed the river. And he passed, passed again, ten, twenty, thirty times - perhaps even after my departure from the river - the military bridge.

I was told by the Carabinieri who were standing sentry at the bridge that they had wanted to prevent him from crossing at dawn. But seeing that he had been a poor madman, out of patriotic joy, they all let him cross the crowded bridge.

For him it was the ecstasy of delight to pass freely, on both sides, the Piave, sure that both banks were finally, as before, his homeland where he could walk proudly, shouting without restraint "Hurrah Italy!"

Isn't he also a patriot? Subjectively, what difference could there be between him who went mad with joy at the liberation of the invaded territory and a soldier who fell smiling under enemy fire?

Love of hearth — Love of country

Imagine, Mr. Senator, a picture of a deserted countryside, on the right, a completely ruined little house, and on the left, a neglected vineyard where the vine shoots stretch out dragging on the ground, like Medusa's hair. Under the bare and cold walls of those staggering remains, an old man and two women dumbly dig up the wreckage of tiles and bricks and carry them away with slow steps. Two children, sitting on a stone, are warming themselves, silent too, in front of a fire, from which a column of whitish smoke rises waving to the grey sky. Beside the children, exposed to the sharp wind of early winter, half-buried by the disrupted hedges, white chrysanthemums bloom in picturesque disorder.

Over the fields, the ruins, the old man, the women, the children, the fire, the flowers, the light, thick rain falls silently,

It is a scene I saw just past the Piave River. I would give this painting a title: "In search of yesterday's hearth."

Love of home is the sacred origin of love of country; don't you think so, Senator?

Liberation

I saw this scene a few hours after the first Italian troops advanced. I was the first bourgeois who had come in the first Italian car. The population, happy with the liberation, ran to meet me and the troops passing by. Everyone was shouting with joy and greeting us like crazy. I too was shouting passionately: "Long live Italy! Long live Italy!"

I felt as if I had found myself in my homeland, back there after an absence of many, many years. The unanimous exaltation of the people was so impressive that they all seemed like my relatives, freed from the tyrannical pillory and the obscure life sentence and now happy to be able to embrace us again and happy to call us brothers.

There were many, especially the old men and women, who cried with joy. In the square of Oderzo ran to me two old women who, taking my hand, kissed it and kissed always crying hard. They could not even say a word, they were so suffocated by the wrong sobs of joy. I couldn't help being moved by this spontaneous outburst and — I don't feel ashamed to tell you — my face was wet with tears that flowed thickly.

That day I fully felt the symbolic solemnity of the flag. My heart leapt at every tricolor waving in the morning breeze. I'm happy to inform you that on that day I never neglected to salute all the tricolor flags raised by the passionate people after a long and painful year of suffering.

Darwinism of greetings

On the subject of greeting, allow me a Manzonian detour. In the early days I would greet carabinieri, sentries, etc. by taking off my hat. However, when I am flying by car, at the moment I have taken it off, I am already a hundred meters away from them. True to the theory of Darwinism, I learned from experience the necessity of the military salute. So here in the war zone, I greet every person with military style.

Farewell caresses

From Oderzo I tried to go to Motta di Livenza, where there was still a patrol of enemies. All the bridges, blown up by them before the hasty escape, forced me to make a very long turn to try to enter Motta from the southeast, instead of directly from the west.

I could say that I was the very first, because I was right after the few cavalrymen and cyclists and before the bersaglieri who had to make an assault on the enemy.

During this tour, I passed a small village that is marked on the map as Palazzo Revedin. The majestic palace of Conte Revedin had been transformed by the enemy into a military hospital. It was just two and a half hours after the

Austrians had escaped. My usual curiosity drove me to the courtyard. I entered a wing where the most seriously ill and wounded had been collected.

The enemy had abandoned them.

In the cold hall, with windows without panes, that let the sharp wind pass freely, lay ten sick and wounded men, groaning. And all of them had only one blanket, with which they covered themselves from head to foot, exposed to the harsh wind.

I approached the first bed, it was an Austrian officer. With a few German words that I knew, I tried to ask for news. But he, always staring into space, like one who is dreaming, answered nothing. The girls in the village let me know that he had not spoken or moved for two days.

Poor abandoned man! He too must have had loved ones anxiously awaiting his return, unaware that their awaited one lay unconscious, dying, neglected and abandoned.

The most terrible of all was the corpse of an Italian lieutenant who, seriously wounded, had been taken prisoner on the Piave, He lay on the floor, half-naked. His chest, back, shoulders and face were full of black spots, covered with mud.— I say mud from the road and not dust from the badly cleaned floor.— He lay slumped in a pool of blood sprayed from his nose.

It was a terrible death. I asked the girls how this poor lieutenant had died.

And they, weeping, told me that the Austrian officers, after having prepared the escape, had entered this room and, having dragged him out of bed and having thrown him on the dusty floor, had given him, together with laughter and mockery, cruel kicks on the face, on the chest, with their muddy shoes and boots.

When the girls came in, trembling like leaves, after the escape of the human hyenas, the poor lieutenant was already dead.

Have you seen that, Mr. Senator?

What beneficent caresses the Austrians gave to a poor wounded Italian! What a vivid contrast between the simple wounded Austrian soldiers who, under the dense bursts of grenades, fraternally cared for a wounded Italian, and the enemy officers who could kick a poor dying wounded man to death.

I have learned that the nobility of the heart does not always correspond to the number of decorations, stars or ribbons that adorn military uniforms.

Shortly thereafter, I removed the blanket from a bed ahead, to ask the sick man a few questions. And — what a surprise! — I found him already cold in Death's hands.

Forty meters from the enemies

Still running south of Motta, I found myself suddenly in front of the enemy.

A Bersaglieri shouted imperiously: "Get down! Get down under the embankment! The enemy is forty meters away."

At this moment, the sinister whistles of rifle bullets passed through the air near me.

I left the car in the courtyard of a peasant house and visited, after dark, the headquarters of the Bersaglieri of the Cosenza Brigade. After the rustic lunch that the commander offered me, I dared to enter Motta on foot, taking advantage of the darkness and making my way in front of the enemy who were so close that when I passed Punico Ponte, which had remained safe across the Livenza, I could hear their voices in the dark.

Along the very long bank of the river, the bersaglieri were impatiently waiting, under the embankment, for the order to assault. And I, exposed to the enemies and protected by the dark sky and accompanied by the whistles of rifles and machine guns, I headed, silent and proud, towards the Motta.

I entered at about 7:30 a.m.

I gathered, directly from the mouths of the people, the news of the terrible oppression of the Austrians and, passing by the house of the mayor completely enveloped in flames, set on fire by the enemies, I returned to Osteria, where I had left the car.

It was absolutely impractical to run on the muddy bank, in the car that makes such a loud noise in the silence of the high night. I left, therefore, the car in the courtyard, woke up the trembling family of the farmer and asked for one evening's hospitality. There was not even a free bed. He led me to the barn under the roof where, throwing myself perfectly dressed, with hat, shoes, gloves, etc.. on the piles of corn straw, I spent an unforgettable night, in the company of rats that jumped gleefully in the dark.

To scare or to tickle

The following day, I left at dawn for Padua.

Near S. Paolo, I saw, on the road, a sign with an austere and funny notice. It says : "Crossing this line is forbidden to civilians — Trespassers will be shot!"

It's pretty, don't you think? I would like to know if, when I saw, for the first time, this threatening poster, I should shudder with fear or burst into laughter.

It has become such a long letter that I am afraid of boring you. I stop here, hoping to be able to write you a much better letter tomorrow.

With warmest regards to you, to S.E. Nitti's family and to Admiral Millo's family.

I salute you in military style,

Yours sincerely
Harukici Shimoi.

LETTER FROM SEN. G. DE LORENZO
Naples, November 9, 1918

Dear Shimoi,

I had your first letter published in the "Mattino", of which I enclose a piece. But this second letter of yours is even more beautiful and interesting.

Continue to write to me in this way, which will give great pleasure to me, to the Nitti family and to the Millo family. Have many, many greetings and good wishes from them and from

Your affectionate
G. De Lorenzo

PADOVA
10 Novembre 1918

Dear Mr. Senator,

On November 3, the glorious day on which the tricolors were seen waving in the skies over Trento and Trieste, I found myself alternately happy in front of the monument to Dante in Italian Trento. It is of those two days, November 3 and 4, which seem to me like a dream, that I want to write to you today. You will already have read, in many newspapers, the long articles that describe in detail the events so fantastic that they would be absolutely incredible to those who have not witnessed them. I hope, however, that you will find in this mine, descriptions that, if they do not carry the figures and names of regiments and brigades etc., as in the newspaper articles. at least present some beautiful scenes that were neglected by the war correspondents.

On November 8, as soon as I had breakfast, I left Padua for Trent. On my chest and on my hat, waved the long ribbons of tricolor.

Of the rest in Verona, — the city that I have longed to visit, for the beautiful memory of the tragic love of Romeo and Juliet and the fierce revenge of Rosmunda and, above all, of Dante's refuge; of the ride north along the Adige to Sega — I write nothing. I will begin from Sega my usual fragmentary narrations.

Beauty of Lagarina valley

The Sorrento peninsula, serene and crowned by olive groves and orange trees, is so enchanting that it seems like a vision; it is of feminine beauty; while Pisola di Capri and the Amalfi coast rise majestically from the blue sea, like the gigantic walls that encircle the gulf of Naples;— is of masculine beauty.

However, when I make the trip, parading among these colorful beauties, first amazed and then fascinated by the magnificent chiseled works of the greatest sculptor Nature, there is always something unspeakable that leaves me, on the return, a little disappointed. Passing now the Lagarina valley, from Sega to Trento, it came to me, like a silver arrow flying in the dark, the revelation of my sadness" Water is missing. I don't mean sea water, which is rather stable, but running water, like rivers, torrents, waterfalls, etc..

"The virtuous love the mountains and the intelligent the water." says Confucius, the great Chinese philosopher, because the mountains are stable and constant while water is mobile and variable. When these stability, constancy and mobility, variability make a perfect harmony, there is an ideal beauty of Nature.

The Lagarina valley is, for this reason, perfectly beautiful. All Japanese would love the Valley, with the dizzying mountains on two sides and the swift Adige in the middle; villages scattered here and there in the woods; castles, monasteries on the peaks of the rocky mountains; niches of the Madonna with sparkling lights and flowers offered by innocent little hands; simple and honest farmers' cottages, where one always finds a cheerful fireplace, good wine, cordial hospitality; pointed bell towers, from which the dulcet bells come swaying over the mist;— all these make up an enchanting view to us Japanese. Lagarina valley is just that.

If I had not been enchanted by the beautiful Neapolitan sky, full of light, life and poetry, I would gladly lead a rustic life in a little house in this valley.

Excuse me, Senator, for my long digression, but this is the essence of my impressions of the trip from Verona to Trent; there is no stink of war, because it was truly a pleasure trip, except for several fires, corpses, long tunnels of masks along the road, and the brake and the headlight of the car, broken during the trip, which made my impatient arrival very late. What delays! I arrived after midnight in Trento,— I repeat emphatically — in Italian Trento.

Napoleonic scenes

I said before that the scenes in Trento on the 3rd and 4th were incredibly fantastic. The car parading in the dark (because the lighthouse was out of order), among the soldiers and prisoners, suddenly found itself at the entrance to the city; and I was amazed and astonished at the stupendous scenes of the high night!

What Napoleonic scenes!

The fields, pastures, roads, gardens, streets and alleys were full of prisoners. Think of 150,000 (some said 200,000) prisoners concentrated in Trent. Confusion, disorder, murmurs, shouts, which covered the illuminated city (I say illuminated as day), seemed like an immense beehive overthrown by the hand of the Invisible. And the sky of the Valley, lying between the black Alps, was illuminated red by the reflection of the innumerable bivouacs that stretched as far as the horizon.

A solemn thing! An incredible thing!

Raucous driving

Like a ship heading out on the rough sea toward the harbor, my car sailed slowly but steadily ahead among the tide of prisoners.

Tana had already passed in the night. As soon as I entered the City that I thought, until that moment, was as dark as a tomb, I saw it dazzlingly illuminated, and the citizens who were still awake caught me with "Hurray!" I wanted to go immediately to Piazza Dante. And I easily found — nay, was offered — a guide, an old gentleman who was running towards me, shouting "Viva l'Italia!" Here I have written "shouting" out of convention, but, if I were to tell the truth, I would not know what word to use, because it was not a shout but was instead, I would say, the shadow of a shout, empty, resembling the murmurs of mosquitoes. It was totally hoarse.

He told me - or rather, he let me know while gesticulating - that, out of extreme joy, he had been screaming continuously all day and evening, unable to eat or sleep because of the excitement.

And he got into his car and drove me to Piazza Dante.

You who knows well how much I love the sweet language of Italy and how much I adore the Supreme Poet, — you can imagine my joy at that moment so solemn that it made me weep. I was finally in Trento (and especially on the day of its Redemption!) in front of the famous monument that has been erected as the symbol of Italianism and of the silent and firm patriotism of the people of Trento.

In front of the monument

Solemn was the moment.

Midnight had already passed. The thin rain came. In the dark sky, the monument rose black and haughty.

And, on the polished marble of its pedestal, knelt and bowed reverently, under the gentle drizzle, a small young man who came from the Far East, leaving his loved ones far away, braving the stormy sea that stretches for five thousand miles, guided only by the love of the divine words of the Poet, like a little bird, lost in the dark, flashes at dawn, across the immense sky, with its wings fully open, towards the first rays of Dawn.

Oh how happy I was, unspeakably happy!

Bivouacs of Piazza Dante

The Piazza was fully occupied by Italian soldiers. Hundreds and hundreds of bivouacs were reflected in the sky, and around them were the soldiers, the liberating officers of the City. Some slept on the ground as if on a royal bed, others talked playfully among merry laughter, while the light night rain fell silently on them all.

Imagine a fantastic camp from the days of the Caesars. Then you will have some idea of the grandiose scene in the Piazza that night.

Imperial Hotel Trento I.

Sentinel

It began to rain heavily.

All the soldiers, the officers, soaked like sponges and, sitting or lying on the wet ground, did not move from their bivouacs, their walking hearths.

Merry chatter.... long laughter.

I wanted to find shelter until dawn. And I headed for the Albergo Imperiale Trento, which the Poet indicated with his right hand.

"HALT!" —a sentry at the entrance.

"Who goes there?"

"I want to rest a little."

"You can not."

"Why?"

"There is a general sleeping area."

"But in this great hotel, there must be hundreds of rooms."

"All are occupied by officers. They are now sleeping peacefully.... And, I tell you, there are also their ladies."

"What!? The ladies? But excuse me, who are these officers!"

"The Austrians."

"Prisoners?"

"Yes sir."

What a pain! Excessive charity! Don't you think so?

The prisoners sleep quietly, like kings, in rooms with all the comforts, in the luxury bed, in the arms of their women, while all the winners sit or lie on the wet ground, uncovered in this rain.

Is this reasonable?

"Prisoner is prisoner, whether officer or general. He must be treated as such. Let me pass. I'll wake them up at once and throw them out."

And an assault on the hotel.

Imperial Hotel Trento II.
Dining Room

I entered the dining room, a very large room where the tables were left all in disorderly bacchanal a dinner just finished. (The prisoners had dinner in the magnificent hall, while the victors contented themselves with a sip of coffee in the rain!)

All the enemy officers slept peacefully everywhere. I highly admire the courageous serenity of the enemies (they are officers!) who can sleep so peacefully, unconcerned about the condition of their homeland, their threatened families and, above all, the shame of surrender, whatever the reason. Did they ignore the pride and dignity of warriors?

I woke them up, one after the other. They looked at me in amazement with sleepy eyes. Then they gathered, little by little, in the antechamber, talking and discussing animatedly among themselves.

I saw, at a table in the middle of the room, two drunken soldiers, sleeping with their heads resting on the table, shivering, or rather, shaking miserably, from the cold or from. despair. I hesitated for a moment to wake these poor soldiers. Thinking, however, of the Italian soldiers who remained outside, wet, I gave, with resolute courage, some shocks to their shoulders.

A sudden burst of sneezing was followed by a sharp voice, which resounded in the hall: — "Jesus! Jesus! Let me sleep!" By Jove! In Neapolitan!

I jumped back, surprised by the flaming eyes, like those of a tiger, that looked at me threateningly. They were two Neapolitan Ardites (more precisely, one from Poggioreale and the other from Salerno) who were keeping watch over the more than two hundred Austrian officers.

These officers, bored of being armed shepherds for these sheep, had taken part in the Neapolitan dinner without compliment and were snoozing happily.

They were truly of the Neapolitan type.

"Did you see that?" I said to them. "The victory is complete. I hope to see you again soon in Naples.... Don't you want to go back to our beautiful Naples soon !"

"Yes... Hunting is good here too."

"Do you have girlfriends?"

"What girlfriends!" (replied the Salernitano, with a wise smile) "A woman is always a heavy chain. It's better to be free. But, you know, if I wanted to be safe, all I have to do is walk down the street of Salerno." He got up suddenly, staggering and took two military steps with his chest sticking out and a beaming smile, superbly showing his open chest and the dagger in front of him. "and I will find a hundred women watching me.... Don't laugh! Word of honour".

"Do you have a father and mother?"

"Yes, even brothers, three; — two are in the army."

"Do you often receive letters from your family?"

"Sometimes; but I always think these letters are annoying, I can't read them. And... I know they're good and that's enough for me. If they are sick, what am I supposed to do?... When a postcard comes, do you know what I do? I look at the figure and throw it; if it's a letter, down a dark hole."

"A dark hole? What for?"

"Unff... toilet paper, do you understand?"

And we, all three of us, burst out in an echoing laughter, in the middle of the enemy officers who looked at us astonished.

Just think, Senator, that everywhere in the hotel there were weapons!

The next morning, I saw, at the Piazza, my cheerful Neapolitan Ardites who were having breakfast, sitting on the freshly wet flower bed. They greeted me They greeted me with a smile, as cordial as young girls. And the one from Salerno gave me, as a souvenir, a dagger belonging to an Austrian officer.

Dawn in the Piazza Dante

Dawn came.

It was no longer raining.

And, like a virgin who bows before the altar, ringed by the long awaited bridegroom, the redeemed Trento throbbed with delight, under the clear veil of the morning mist.

Christmas and carnival

Around seven in the morning, in Piazza Dante, a highly picturesque scene spontaneously unfolded, which, unfortunately, was overlooked by the war correspondents.

They told me that, in the Trento Hotel, there used to be the headquarters of an army. The square was literally covered with all kinds of papers abandoned by the enemy and there were piles of papers everywhere.

Suddenly, in a corner of the square, some cheerful soldiers began to joke, throwing the cards among themselves, as the boys enjoy, in winter, throwing snowballs. At once this childish jest spread epidemically among the soldiers who filled the Square. Some found a quantity of the rolls of telegraphic paper and began to throw it in the air, through the telegraphic wires, the branches of the trees, making it in a few minutes the decoration of the whole Square, as at the day of a great feast. The white ribbons of the telegraph paper waved and swayed, straight, from wire to wire, from tree to tree. And I, who love all children's games, was running happily, throwing the paper in the air along with these innocent bearded children.

To the group of soldiers who were playing with me, I shouted out loud: "To celebrate the liberation of Trento, look! Christmas and Carnival have come early together." The spiraling trees, with ribbons thickly hanging from the branches, looked exactly like the

Christmas Tree, while, in the air, white, red and blue cards were flying everywhere, just like at Carnival.

The proud soldiers who remain motionless in front of the bursts of grenades, played that morning like five year old children, running, falling, jumping and shouting playfully in Neapolitan, Tuscan, Sicilian, Lombard, Venetian, in various dialects of theirs (which are all children of their father's language), while the Supreme Father of the Italic language, extended his hand over them, as if he wanted to bless them, that they promptly rushed to join with another brotherly dialect: Trentino.

Full of tricolor

The City was extraordinarily full of life and movement— movement of the liberating troops, of dull prisoners, of exalted citizens. And all these movements were covered by the waving of innumerable tricolors that covered the whole town, while ribbons of tricolors decorated the chests of all the citizens.

I don't understand how and where the population of an Austrian city (at least politically) until yesterday had such a large number of flags and tricolor ribbons ready.

Together with the merit of the Italian troops who, with a lightning march, rushed to achieve the redemption of the City, for which so many martyrs offered, smiling and confident, their lives, and the valiant napoleonic deeds of the enemy army of one hundred and fifty thousand soldiers who were able to perform, without shame, a surrender so ready and unanimous, I can not help but admire the ardent and constant aspiration of the citizens who had always ready, under the threat of the Austrian sword, such an enormous amount of tricolors.

Public thieves

I wanted to visit the castle where Battisti was hanged as a saint. I left and climbed a hill to the south outside the city, which, I later learned, was Stradone.

I am happy to remember that, in those solemn and agitated days, the city order was splendidly maintained by the few old patriots, dressed as bourgeois and armed with Austrian weapons abandoned in the street. They all wore large tricolor ribbons on their chests.

When I saw, for the first time, one of these protectors of the population, an old man with white hair, I asked him who he was. "National Guard! "he replied haughtily.

Beautiful is the word national. With this word Nation, the proud old man certainly meant Italy.

Party at City Hall

I was informed that, at the Town Hall, the ceremony of the delivery of the flag of the Italian city, to Trento redeemed, would take place.

I drove to the Town Hall.

The street was completely filled with the crowd, crazy with enthusiasm. Crossing this dense multitude was a walk of several minutes.

And during this crossing, the enthusiastic citizens buried every passerby with deafening "Hurrah!" When I found myself among the thunders of joy, I, too, stood up in the car and waving my hat, answered them, in a very loud voice, with continuous "Hurrah" I am not ashamed to say that, after this pleasantly strenuous crossing, I was completely hoarse.

In the hall of the Town Hall, greeted by a unanimous "Hurrah" the flag was......Enough! stop! The description of the ceremony and the list of illustrious and not illustrious names who attended it are the stuff of a reporter. I don't want and I can't bore you with the usual journalistic narration that you can find, almost every day, in the columns of "Cronaca della Citta" of any newspaper.

Piedigrotta tridentina

At the time when I was about to leave Trento, I met, by one way, the patriotic demonstration of the population. The young people, the women, the boys, some on foot and the others on wagons, marched triumphantly, singing and shouting .. And the procession lengthened every moment with people who spontaneously joined on all sides. Flags, ribbons, banners, flowers, among the shouts, songs, noises of all kinds such as trumpets, drums, brass bands, oil cans, basins and so on. Many beat the boxes of Austrian masks and helmets that were found, in abundance, everywhere on the street.

The world-famous Piedigrotta festival that I could not see in the Neapolitan city, I finally admired—unexpectedly—in the distant city of Tre Colli, far away by land but close at heart.

Three currents

That day — November 3, 1918, the day of the glory of Italy, which we will remember proudly, as our posterity will remember forever — that day, three parallel currents, resembling a colossal ribbon of tricolor, inseparably linked Trento to Verona; the newborn City of Italy rejoined to the Ancient Italian City of love.

The first of these currents, which descended to the south, was the Adige, which, instead of rushing agitatedly, as in years and years past, with murmurs of indignation and whispers of conspiracy, was now running, throbbing with jubilation and eager to make the Italians participate in the jubilant jubilation of their Tridentine brothers.

The second current of the medium that ran from north to south, was the endless column of prisoners, who were sent down from Trent. I say sent and not led because there was no Italian soldier leading them. Instead, at the concentration camps of departure, several Italian soldiers with whips in their hands… A crack of the whip and an imperious cry: "Up! forward!"

The prisoners get up and start, one after the other, to walk or limp, bent over under the sack. At the arrival concentration camps, other Italian soldiers give them: "Halt! Stop!" and they stop and throw these countless lousy sheep on the ground. The column automatically continues to walk.

During the very long walk, there was no escort. They could escape at any point. There were abandoned weapons and ammunition everywhere... They could have easily rebelled. But the enemies are very wise, because they understand well that it is not convenient for them to be shot for rebelling or to flee to their homeland full of revolution and famine, refusing the warm hospitality of Italy that invited them to a holiday in the Eden of Europe until the day of Peace.

Poor Italy! that must think about making the 150,000 new sudden guests eat and sleep!

The third current that ran hastily and impatiently, from south to north, was that of the Italian troops. Let's tell the truth frankly. It was not a serious military march, as I have always seen in the war zone so far, of the dumb and proud soldiers, but it was, let's say, a festive procession.

The soldiers laughed, sang and shouted, in response to the "Hurrah" of the population. However, Mr. Senator, you should not imagine a line of gray-green military clothing, but rather a living column that stretches endless for a hundred kilometers, white white, interrupted every so often by the dots of tricolor: numerous flags waving in the hands of soldiers. I say white, because there were no soldiers, no horses, no carts, no trucks, but, instead, all were covered entirely by white chrysanthemum flowers. And the soldiers, horses, camions, wagons walked happily under the fragrant loads. It was a column of flowers marching.

Gifts, not contraband

At the beginning, I believed that these romantic soldiers, exalted by some uncontrollable joy, had plundered the gardens of noble villas and the vegetable gardens of peasant houses along the road. However, as soon as I passed them, I understood that their fragrant ammunition, which I had believed until now to be the booty collected by the fierce hands, were, instead, gifts from the gentle hands.

Along the road, at every village, the children, the boys, the girls threw flowers and flowers and flowers to the troops passing by.

Fragrant snowfall

In Verona, the flowers flying from balconies and windows became thicker. And, among the more numerous tricolors and the more enthusiastic hurrahs and under the incessant fragrant snowfall, troops, carriages, automobiles and festively dressed citizens passed by.

When I was outside Verona, my car was almost full of flowers.

Ambush discovered

Having come out safe and sound from the fierce shootings of the flowers in the city of Verona, I flew in hasty flight towards S. Martino of the picturesque bell tower. A little before the town... oh, what terror! here was another ambush... an ambush uncovered!

There were six or seven flourishing young girls who were armed with flowers in their arms. A frightening quantity!

When my car approached them, fleeing at full speed, the Ardite girls with their breasts closed launched themselves into an assault in the middle of the street and behold! A siege of a graceful ferocity; a deafening salvo of "Long live Italy!" bursts of laughter; hand grenades of flowers thrown without respite; lots and lots of delicious stabs on the chest, shoulders, knees, and arms, with chrysanthemum branches, which finally reached the head. They literally covered me with flowers.

And with another chorus of "Hurrah!" they went off triumphantly to their place of ambush, to wait for another lucky victim who will pass this way.

I did not feel the courage to throw away these flowers: the most poetic gift I have ever had in my life. I flew the car loaded with flowers. People on the street were shouting: "Look! Look! Car of flowers!" I doubt if they realized that buried alive in the flowery tomb was a Japanese man who was so happy that he felt he was in a sweet dream.

So I arrived in Padua, where the car, full of flowers, drove into the middle of the procession of the patriotic demonstration that was passing, at that moment, in front of the Press Office, bathed in the red rays of the majestic sunset.

No blood or bodies. No stench of war. They were two days of such poetic delight that I have never experienced before.

When I left Rome, I wanted to see the Piave front, together with Montello, Grappa, Asiago, Pasubio and Adamello. At the beginning of the offensive, I hoped to be able to cross the Piave, maybe just once. After two or three days, my desire widened and I wanted to see, if possible, the water of the Tagliamento.

The victory, in just a few days, flared up, without limit, like the fire that engulfs the vast steppe of America. Now what a Tagliamento! It's just a little river suckling the fertile plain of Tenete. What a Pasubio! What a Adamello! It is an ordinary mountaineering excursion.

What should I see? What country should I visit for the last time on my long tour of the Italian front f I thought and thought and finally I chose two: either Trieste or Caporetto. - To abandon myself in the jubilation of unanimous joy, in Trieste which, together with Trent, was the objective of the long and high aspiration of the Italian nation, or in Caporetto, to renew the painful memory of the blow so cowardly given and the new jubilation of the revenge so nobly and so gloriously accomplished, Either the trip of joy or the trip of tears.

But when? I don't know exactly. Therefore, I cannot say when I will be in Naples, but in the meantime, together with the family of S.E. Nitti, I offer my warmest congratulations on Italy's great victory,

Your Excellency
Harukici Shimoi

SCIMOI

One rainy evening in the winter of 1911, I met Harukici Shimoi.

An illegible note from Gioachino Brognoligo wanted to introduce me to him. But they recognised each other in return, and immediately our two young souls clutched together, trembling with wonder and love. I remember a corrected print of Via Rettifilo with a sofa, a table and a shelf of books. Shimoi, who had not been able to decipher the hieroglyphic writing of our presenter, after looking at me for a while through his shiny double lenses, stood up and approached the bookshelf. It was the only level on which our souls could then adhere. Shimoi spoke Italian badly at that time. Every word came out of his brain and teeth in a spasm of laceration.

"These ones... Japanese classics— he showed me— these... modern poets— and the beautiful tissue editions of silk or paper, bound with a strange elegance and animated with flowers and birds, passed before my eyes.... curious and discontented— everything was so imaginative in there and my heart was so thirsty that even the obscure characters and complicated ideograms took on a life of their own for me that evening,

At the top of the pages, swarms of blue herons took flight and with the paddling of their wings rained the quiet night on all things; cherry-blossomed trees shed their pink petals along enchanting rivieras; small, flat boats swayed strangely in mysterious giant flowers; vine-shoots with wide, autumn-blooded vine-branches unfolded in sumptuous festoons; and far, far away, a mysterious, snow-covered, extinct volcano towered its canines in the sky.

Over all this world of fantasy, printed in a minor tone on the pages of books, climbed the black scarabs of ideograms. And these were the love poems that we had to enjoy together afterwards and revive in our speech.

I soon returned to see him and the second time he read to me and translated in his own way the first poem by Akiko Yosano. A woman, he told me, who is as famous in Japan as Dante is in Italy, even though she is still alive and young.

The poem was too rapid, too luminous for me not to feel its full enchantment at once.

The young autumn is like a salon in the palace, for in it the trees, the birds, the flowers and all other things are plated with gold.

I immediately thought of a translation, and Shimoi clapped his hands in joy. We would have hugged and kissed if we had not been suspicious of our different natures.

From that time on, I returned almost every evening to his room and after a fortnight I brought him the first issue of my Diana with Akiko's sixteen first poems, nimble and fresh in the magazine's wide, soft pages.

Shimoi wanted to read them carefully syllable by syllable, following the line with his finger and marking the most difficult words with his fingernail. His eyes sparkled with joy and his hands trembled. I, too, was moved; more by that young foreigner who was in love with our homeland and had come from so far away on a pilgrimage of love to learn our language and penetrate the mysteries of our greatest poet, than by the publication of the few exotic poems in my young magazine.

Because truly Shimoi is a living miracle of love for our land and our culture.

Ever since he had the light of knowledge, he tried with all his might to approach our distant soul through the universe of Dante.

He recounts with a strange religion that he knew our poet first in the Gardener's edition, then in Cary's translation and finally in the more lyrical one by the poet Longfellow.

He tells of having, after graduating, created in Tokyo a Dantean society in which the liveliest and most restless young people of Japanese society, sacred philosophers, professors and journalists participated. It was a gathering of scholars who sought by every means to penetrate the mystery of Dante's realms. But no one knew Italian and the English translations and commentaries were certainly not faithful and sufficient.

So Shimoi first thought of learning our language so that one day he could read the poem in pure Italian to his fellow workers.

He has not left this joy and toil for more than ten years. He spent the first six or seven in his homeland and they are of dark eve, the last three or four he has spent here in Naples and running all over Italy.

Now not only can he read Dante to his companions in Tokyo, but he can also enjoy all of our later poetry and, what is more difficult, the restless and suffered contemporary poetry.

Now not only does he speak and write Italian with sufficient correctness, but he also gives essays of vernacular competence that are so rude and certain as to stop and chill even on the Neapolitan carriages our loquacious and mannered coachmen. Shimoi is truly a living phenomenon of love.

He is a young man of lively and modern genius whom I am proud to have met before anyone else in Italy.

A house that has had all its paper walls sliding around in the cheerfulness of the morning is not, as one might think, flooded with light, but light with shadows and coolness.

They say the nights are wider down there too.

On one wall of my room an old Japanese legend unfolds its bizarre figures in a precious painting: a young woman with a light scroll unfolded advances on high hooves in the diffuse moonlight. The stars do not tremble on high, rivers do not flow through the fields in the immense cycle, from all the details around it rains and pours forth such pure kindness, such a cosmic sense of things that moves and enchants.

I have often been out and about with Shimoi, and as far as my mountain he came on a peaceful Easter, but I have never seen him stopped by a heroic spectacle, never lost in the vast and solemn lines.

The whole universe lights up in a trembling drop of dew.

A superb and powerful rock has all its value for Shimoi gathered in the pale corolla, of a little flower that from a cleft swings on the edge of the last wind. And even the Alps I think are worth to him in function of the velvet edelweis.

So it happened one day that when Shimoi arrived at the Italian front to learn about our war, he didn't want to know about the accurate organisations, the patient plans, the hard-won achievements; but only the diffuse and invisible soul did he care about, that kindness and poetry that others perhaps missed and certainly did not think too much about.

He asked to be present at the distribution of mail in the camp to catch the shining tremors of emotion in the frank eyes of our soldiers, and in return the command officers wasted their time unravelling the tangle of our wartime postal services before him.

He wanted to catch the first convulsive words from the lips of our humble wounded in the line of fire, but instead the others took him around the rear hospitals and enlightened him with generous expertise.

But the others were our senior officers and they had good reason to act in such a way, even if Shimoi may appear justifiably grief-stricken to the more sophisticated.

The others were the officers fighting with the enemy or with evils, consumed by four years of ardour and dazzled by a single noble light.

This is one of the thousands of times when right and wrong cannot be cut with the thread of judgement into two clean and decisive slices.

By the time Shimoi got up there, our senior officers and our fighters were so saturated with pure and great episodes that they could no longer distinguish them with any certainty or feel any difference between them. Their unlikely lives were all one endless episode of anguish and poetry, and it must have seemed to them a curious individual who still managed to take an interest in a humble, brave soldier who takes in and cares for a small, lost dog under the bombardment.

I don't know what will be said about this book in which Shimoi has collected his impressions of our war. A few months ago, I read a fragment of it in a local newspaper and was surprised by the way Shimoi treated the elements of his emotions. The stylistic uncertainty, the syntactic perplexity, push the author into a dangerous game of balances and recklessness, into a round of arbitrary and alarming constructions that are a wonder and an enchantment and are enough in themselves to reveal in this young foreigner, not yet master of our language, a brilliant and modern artist of the first quality.

I, who edited this book, have tried never to alter Shimoi's straightforward expression, which is therefore all and only his.

Giuseppe de Lorenzo wanted to make it even more precious with the gift of his own introduction.

The various things that are interwoven in the text, the pages of Gabriele d'Annunzio, the letters of Francesco Nitti, de Lorenzo, Civinini and others, are not put in here for the sake of vanity, but constitute and mark necessary moments of lived action which, to be such, are inherent in the action itself.

Even these words of mine, fraternally requested by Shimoi, are more an act of love than a usual justification.

But that is enough.

A Japanese legend says that at the bottom of the South Sea, on the side of Linscioten, between the submerged reefs of four beautiful islands, lies the enchanted castle of the mysterious King of the Waters.

The algae and deep corals make a restless garden around it. The sun can be seen in the distance as a vague emerald orb, which the foam of the sea surface mists up and laces around like pale cirrus clouds.

The mysterious King of the waters is a tremendous dragon who, in the enchanted castle, guards a daughter of extraordinary beauty.

Legend has it that the young Urascima, the son of a poor fisherman who had fallen in love with her, and the ancient and noble national hero Tauara Tóda, invited by the Dragon King, were able to descend to the bottom of the sea to see this divine prisoner.

But the marvellous maiden is still at the bottom of the southern waters, and in vain do men come from all the islands around, from the villages on the mainland, and plunge into the quiet and treacherous gulf to inebriate themselves with her smile.

Who can ever liberate it?

Is it not our poetry? The one so long sought after in the depths of our heart?

And whoever has once managed, even from far away, to catch a single glimmer of her shining eyes and to bring it intact among men, as a gift of kindness, is he not worthy above all of our heartfelt love?

Gherardo Marone

Lightning Source UK Ltd.
Milton Keynes UK
UKHW012027130223
416963UK00009B/161